# Grandma's Gift

## Eric Velasquez

Walker & Company
New York

Aa
Bb
Cc

"*¡Feliz Navidad, Eric!*" My teacher walked me to the classroom door, where my grandmother was waiting to take me back to her apartment for my winter break. I used to spend all my school vacations with her so she could take care of me while my parents worked.

Before we left, my teacher handed Grandma a note about our holiday project. The Metropolitan Museum of Art had just bought a famous painting, and I had to go see it and write a report.

On our way home, Grandma asked me to translate the note because she couldn't read English. I'd translate a lot of things for Grandma—sometimes I felt like I was going to school for two. All the note said was, "Metropolitan Museum of Art, 82nd Street and Fifth Avenue, Second Floor, New Exhibit."

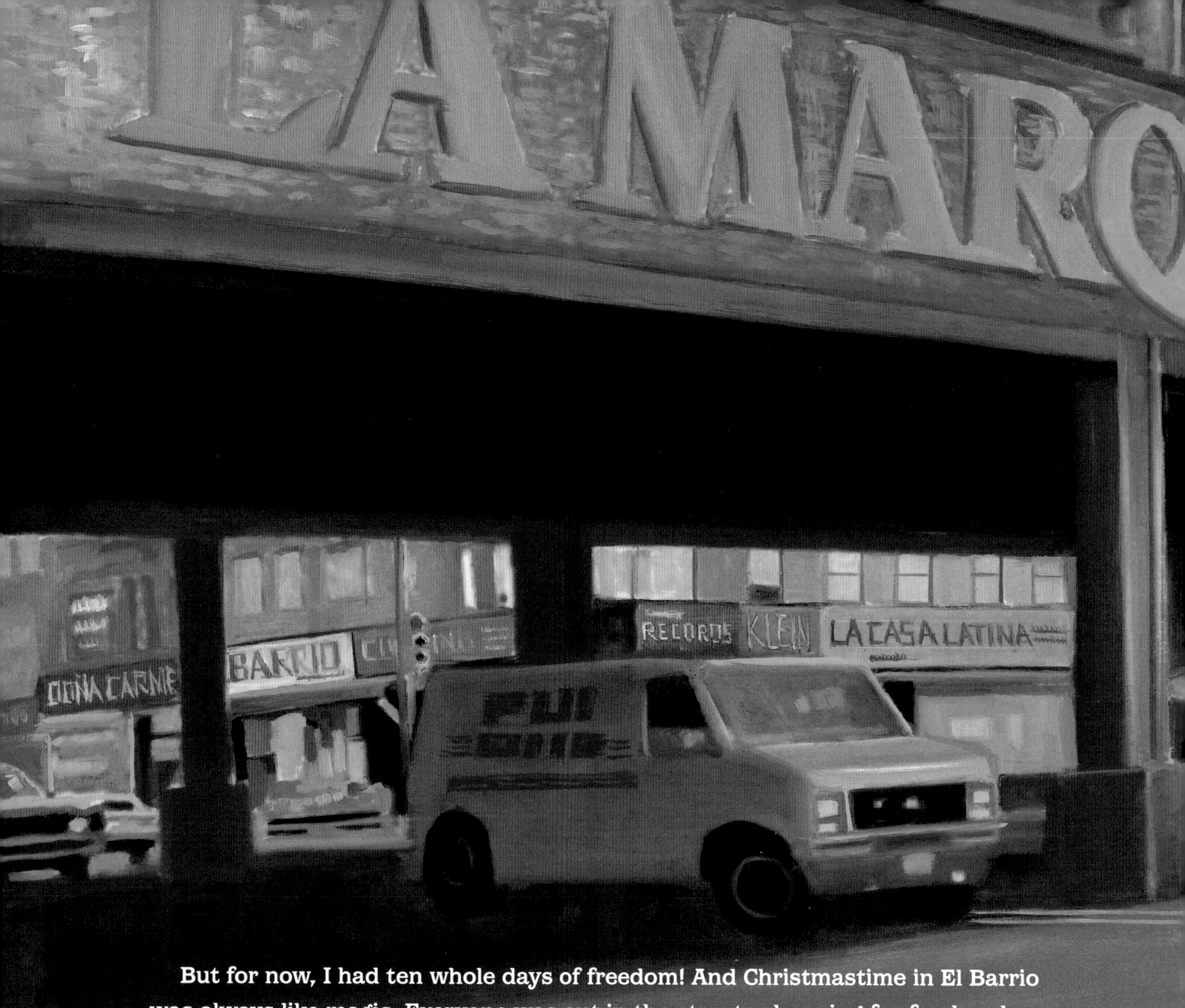


But for now, I had ten whole days of freedom! And Christmastime in El Barrio was always like magic. Everyone was out in the streets shopping for food and gifts, and Grandma was ready to join them. So we dropped off my suitcase and headed straight to La Marqueta (the market)—one of my favorite places.

This special group of shops and stalls sat under the elevated train tracks, and all the stalls rumbled and shook whenever a train passed overhead.

UETA
115

FRESH
FISH
98¢
83¢
1.29

Grandma could find everything she needed there year-round—fruits, vegetables, fish, meat, clothing, and even her favorite records. But that day, Grandma was shopping only for the ingredients for *pasteles*, the traditional Christmas dish for Puerto Ricans. She promised that if I helped her make the *pasteles* this year, she would take me to the museum.

Our first stop was the produce stand to buy the root vegetables.

*"Estoy buscando calabaza, yautía, plátanos verdes, guineos verdes y papas,"* Grandma said to the first vendor. (I'm looking for pumpkins, taro root, green plantains, green bananas, and potatoes.)

*"Pues aquí tenemos los mejores."* (Well, here are the best.) All the vendors knew that Grandma would buy only the best ingredients for her famous *pasteles*.

When they agreed on the price, Grandma said, *"¡Gracias, y Feliz Navidad!"* (Thank you, and Merry Christmas!)

PRODUCTOS
20

Our next stop was the butcher stand.

*"¿Cuál pedazo le gusta, Doña Carmen?"* Alberto asked. (Which piece do you like, Miss Carmen?)

*"Se ve bueno. Dame cuatro libras,"* Grandma said. (That one is good. Give me four pounds.)

After that, our last stop was Doña Juanita's bodega for parchment wrapping paper, banana leaves, string, and El Barrio's latest gossip.

The worst part of the trip was carrying the heavy shopping bags up five flights of stairs to Grandma's apartment. As soon as she took off her coat, Grandma headed straight to the kitchen and went right to work peeling and grating the root vegetables by hand—never with a blender.

"If you want it to taste traditional, you must make it traditionally," she always said.

When I asked her where she learned to grate so fast, she only answered, "You should have seen my mother grate."

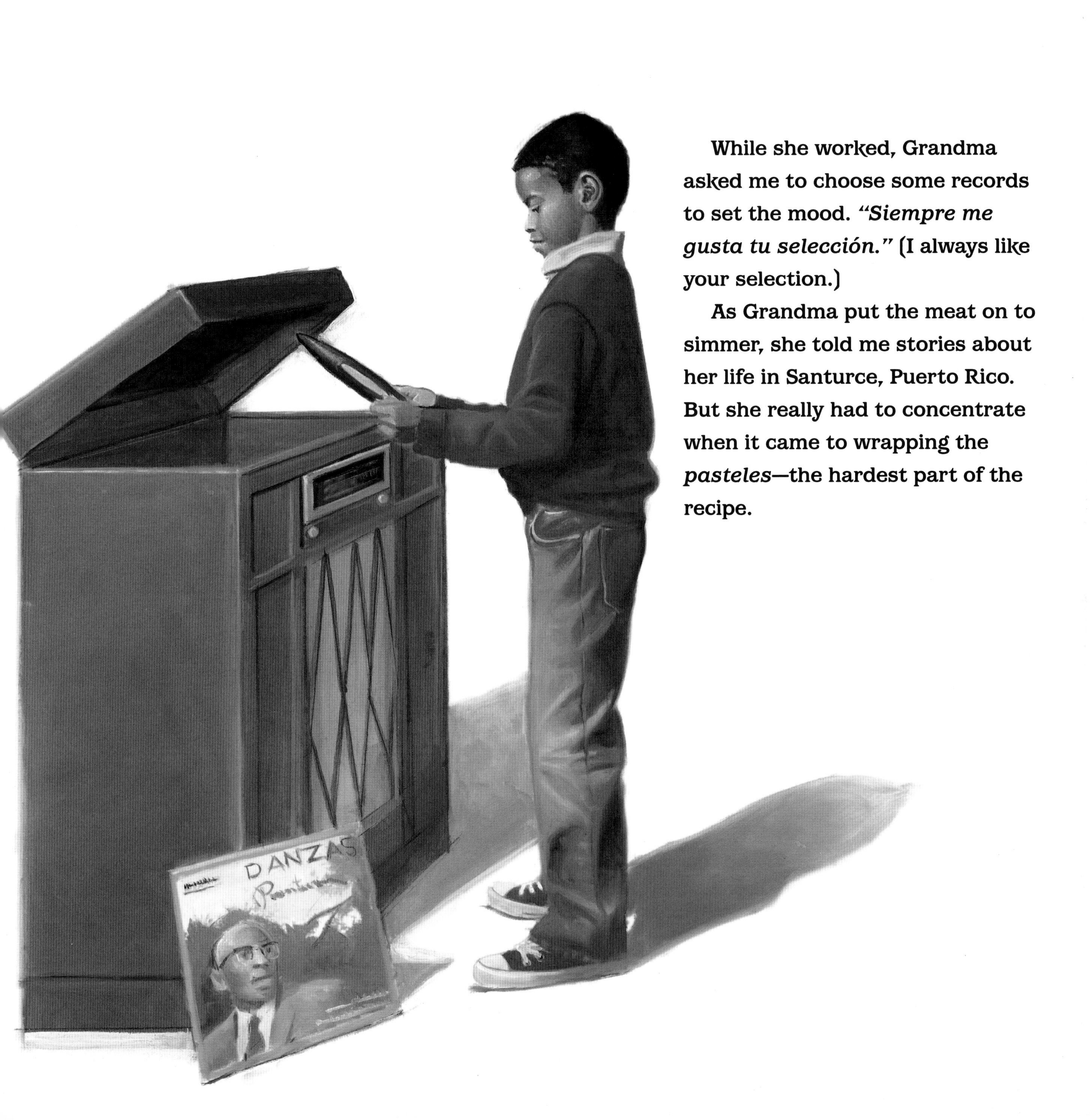


While she worked, Grandma asked me to choose some records to set the mood. *"Siempre me gusta tu selección."* (I always like your selection.)

As Grandma put the meat on to simmer, she told me stories about her life in Santurce, Puerto Rico. But she really had to concentrate when it came to wrapping the *pasteles*—the hardest part of the recipe.